AUNT DEE

T0019810

AUNT DEE

Stacy Davis

TATE PUBLISHING
AND **ENTERPRISES, LLC**

The opinions expressed by the author are not necessarily those of Tate Publishing, LLC.

Published by Tate Publishing & Enterprises, LLC
127 E. Trade Center Terrace | Mustang, Oklahoma 73064 USA
1.888.361.9473 | www.tatepublishing.com

Tate Publishing is committed to excellence in the publishing industry. The company reflects the philosophy established by the founders, based on Psalm 68:11,
"The Lord gave the word and great was the company of those who published it."

Book design copyright © 2014 by Tate Publishing, LLC. All rights reserved.
Cover design by Joseph Emnace
Interior design by Gram Telen
Illustrations by Noelle Barcelo

Published in the United States of America

ISBN: 978-1-62994-692-4
1. Fiction / Short Stories
2. Juvenile Fiction / Social Issues / Death & Dying
13.12.10

To my brothers, who care.

CHAPTER 1

Aunt Dee was sixty-two years old when she died, and I swear you ain't never seen such a beautiful smile on a lady who was dead. Heck, you probably ain't never seen such a beautiful smile on a lady who was livin'. She had teeth the color a' cotton that filled her entire mouth, every speck, and every time she smiled her lips stretched out ear to ear so as everyone could see all her teeth. Now if that ain't contagious, nothin' is.

She was smilin' this smile at her funeral. Real big and full of life. Not the way you'd think a woman would be at her own funeral. Usually dead people are stone cold. Stiff as a board. Lifeless lookin, ya know? But not Aunt Dee. You ain't never seen such a beautiful, lively smile on a woman at her own funeral.

There was one person who wasn't smilin at the funeral though, and that was my daddy. My daddy ain't smiled since my mama died, and the truth is I feel like every time he looks at me the pain in his face gets worse. I can't figure out why, I mean I don't look like her or nothin', not like other daughters and mamas do, but he still can't look at me with joy in his eyes. Hasn't for years. And I know it's because... oh, never mind. It doesn't matter now.

He had that same painful look burnin' in his eyes at the funeral. There he sat, my daddy, in the very last row, three chairs in from the isle. He sat there and stared at the ground. I shoulda went and hugged him, right? Shoulda told him I was sorry the only woman in his life he loved as much as Mama was dead now too. But I couldn't. I couldn't because anytime I so much as looked at him, the pain in his eyes turned to hate. My daddy hated me now, and I knew he would never forgive me. When you're sixteen years old, forgiveness is hard thing to understand. Heck- when you're sixty years old forgiveness is a hard thing to understand. The only person I ever knew who understood what forgiveness meant was Aunt Dee, and now here I was feelin' stone cold and heartbroken standing on the stage at her funeral while my daddy stared at the ground in the back pew. The soft melody of Amazing Grace played in the background, and I thought one more time about how Aunt Dee was the only person I knew who understood forgiveness. She was the only person who forgave me for my momma dyin', and she tried to tell my daddy—but he just couldn't understand. I glanced at Aunt Dee one final time as people were being ushered in. I just stared, and tried to soak in that smile. I even found myself

tryin' to draw life from that smile like I had so many times before—but with Aunt Dee no longer breathin', I couldn't find the life I was lookin' for. I closed my eyes and tried to imagine Aunt Dee, alive and full. Full of laughter, and joy and forgiveness. I remembered what she said to me the day I lost my mama, *"Ain't no one's job but God's to take a life…"*

A warm tear swelled in my right eye. As hard as I tried to keep it locked in, the second I opened my eyes it came runnin' down my cheek. I couldn't hide the tears any longer. Aunt Dee was gone forever and there was no one left to forgive me.

I quickly ducked behind the thick black curtain on stage so no one would see me cryin', at least not yet. The music softly faded away and I could hear the preacher's loud footsteps pound their way across the stage. It was time. I knew I couldn't hide any longer so I took one more deep breath, rubbed the underneath of my eyes real hard to get rid of any smeared makeup, and headed for my seat. I was sittin' in the front row thanks to Big Henry, Aunt Dee's husband—or widower, I suppose. Big Henry knew how much I hated bein' looked at, which is why he was always pushin' me out of the comfortable little box I had lived in all my life.

I'll never forget the first time he made me step out of that box—or more so pushed me right out of it. It was the day before my mama died, that might be why I

remember it like it was yesterday. Either that or I was so embarrassed that the moment was burned into my mind forever. I was nine years old. It was early August in the small town of Dunnsville, Mississippi, and I remember how the sweat felt runnin' down my boney chest and the way my bangs stuck to my forehead.

All I wanted to do that Saturday was eat a box of grape popsicles and run through the sprinkler. This was somethin' I could only do when Aunt Dee and Big Henry was around though cause my daddy didn't like me stompin' holes in the lawn. He didn't mind if I ran the hose on the driveway, but it wasn't the same. I loved the feel of the green grass ticklin' the inside of my toes and the way the lawn got all slippery after the sprinkler had been runnin' for hours on end. And since this particular Saturday my daddy was helpin' Uncle Jim put up a new fence, I knew the lawn would be all mine. Mama had a hair appointment at noon so she asked Aunt Dee and Big Henry if they could come watch me for a few hours. I knew I was old enough to not need a babysitter, but havin' Aunt Dee and Big Henry around was like havin' friends over instead of havin' a babysitter. Plus it really was havin' a friend over when they brought Stretch along. Sometimes he would have to stay home and finish his chores, but most days they watched me he'd get to come. Stretch was Aunt Dee and Big Henry's only son. He was two years older than me, but he always treated me like we were the very same person. I was never little-ole Sheryl to him—I was just Sheryl. And he would include me in all his adventures the same way he'd include anybody else. This same day—the day before my mama died and the day Big Henry pushed me—was the day I knew I loved Stretch. Not just cause' he had dreamy blue eyes and I forgot where I was when he smiled at me, but because he had a beautiful soul.

It was a quarter til noon, and while my mama was frantically runnin' around tryin' to find her purse and keys, I heard the old rickety tires on Big Henry's Chevy come rollin' down the driveway. At this point I would have run upstairs to put my swim suit on, but I already had it on—it was the first thing I did when I woke up. I was hidin' it, of course, under a baggy tshirt and some cutoff jeans, but I was suited up and ready to hit the sprinkler as soon as Mama left. Hearin' Big Henry's tires made me want to throw my shirt off and meet them at the end of the drive, but I knew I needed to be patient. Mama would want to say hi and visit for a few minutes and I definitely didn't want to blow my cover. So there I sat at the kitchen table, swingin' my legs back and forth and sippin' on a glass of lemonade when Big Henry, Aunt Dee and Stretch came in through the screen door. They never bothered to knock, and as soon as they were inside Big Henry hollered out, "Your purse is in the mud room, Caitlin!" as if he already knew she was lookin' for it. She ran into the mud room with a relieved look on her face and gave Big Henry and hug worthy of his size.

"Oh, thank you! I have been lookin' everywhere for this darn thing!"

As she grabbed it and threw it over her shoulder, Aunt Dee and Stretch made their way through the door.

"You headin' off so soon, honey?" Aunt Dee asked, even though she already knew the answer.

"Yes, sorry. I'm already late! Not that Suzzie would care, I'm probably her only appointment today…"

What was Mama standin' around gabbin' for? She needed to leave! The sprinkler was callin'!

"Oh I'm only kiddin', you get goin'. Suzzie will be itchin' to hear some new gossip!"

Thank heavens Aunt Dee was helpin' me rush Mama out the door. I gave her a little nudge in the form of a hug and tried to shove her out.

"Good grief, Sheryl! I didn't know you wanted me gone that badly."

Stretch caught my eye and we both laughed. He already knew what I was wantin', and he wanted it just as bad. I could see his swim trunks peakin' out from under his gym shorts.

"Oh she's just anxious to play, honey. You get goin' and let these kids have some fun!"

With that, my mama was out the door and Stretch and I were running full force to the bathroom so we could strip off our real clothes, grab towels, and run out into the front yard.

"You two better slow down!" hollered Aunt Dee. "Life ain't no fun when you rushin' everywhere…"

Her words were faint and disappeared behind our busy minds as we hustled out the front door.

"Turn it on, Stretch! Turn it on!" I yelled at him to turn on the water, hoping my loud voice would make him go faster. I grabbed the hose and yanked it as hard as I could, giving us plenty of slack to throw the sprinkler around. Just as I went to place it in the middle of the yard, water shot up out of the cold, yellow metal and hit me right in the face. The hose water was so cold it took my breath away, and I completely lost my balance. As I fell to the ground soaking wet, Stretch ran over to where I was laying laughin' so hard I thought he was goin' to fall over himself.

"That…was….so…mean!" I yelled in between gapping breaths.

"Oh, no sir! You loved it!" he laughed again. Soon both of us were laughin' as the water continued to shoot up into the air and get us both wet. By the time we were able to stand up again, Big Henry was bringin' us our first round of popsicles.

"You two are somethin' else" he said as he threw us the frozen plastic tubes. We each grabbed one, not needing to fight over the flavor since they were both blue, and

Big Henry and Aunt Dee pulled up two lawn chairs to set up a safe distance away and watch us have fun.

After what seemed like fifteen minutes had passed, Aunt Dee hollered out that it was time for us to put on some more sun screen.

"It's been two hours, kids, and ain't no child of mine gonna get sunburned. So get your little hineys over here and put on more lotion!"

When Aunt Dee used the word "hiney" we knew she meant business. We both sighed, then started our slow walk over to the sun screen. Big Henry got up to get us more popsicles, and that's about the only thing that made the sun screen trip bearable. Right away, Stretch stuck out his arms and let Aunt Dee slather sun screen all over his pale white skin. She yanked his shorts down just low enough to make me blush and make sure he was good and covered in all areas. This was somethin' that never bothered Stretch, but the older I got the more I wished Aunt Dee wouldn't embarrass us in front of each other like that—or at least not embarrass me.

"Stick out your arms, girl," she ordered.

I slowly lifted my arms, not caring if she did my stomach, but before I knew it she was yankin' on my top like she always did tryin' to pull it off. For the first time in my life, my hands came up to hers and I stopped her.

"Aunt Dee, just my arms and stomach is good enough don't ya think?"

She wasn't understandin' my embarrassment.

"Oh hush child, and let me make sure you're all covered…"

She tried to yank my top off one more time but I stopped her again. I didn't even really mean to, it just happened…

Right as I forcefully stopped her the second time, a chain of events took place that I will never forget.

Big Henry walked back outside with our popsicles, and three local middle school boys rode by our front yard on their bikes—who were of course all friends with Stretch.

"Hey, Stretch!" hollered out Nollan, the "king" of the bunch.

"Oh, hey dude," Stretch said in such a casual way that I wondered if he even knew what it meant to feel embarrassed.

As soon as those boys rode up, I wanted to die. Here Aunt Dee was tryin' to pull my swim top off and three of the cutest boys in town were standing just feet away. I must have turned red as a beet because my face instantly felt like a furnace and Big Henry got a sly, squirrely smile stretchin' across his face.

Oh no. What is he gonna do…

For the third time that day, my chest was poundin'.

"Well howdy there, boys, how ya'll doin'?"

The boys all smiled sheepishly at Big Henry, afraid of his size, and replied as politely as they knew how.

"Oh, uh… good. Doing good, sir, thank you."

"That's real great, good. You boys out ridin' your bikes today?"

"Yes, sir. To the gas station for a soda. It's hot today." They were relaxin' a little now and one of them even stepped off his bike.

Oh I just wish they would leave!

I could still feel my face burning, and I had my hand tightened across Aunt Dee's, who was still pullin' at my top.

"Well that sounds terrific! I bet Stretch and Sheryl would love to come with you boys, wouldn't ya?"

Stretch got such a huge smile. I think he forgot the sprinkler was even on.

"You bet I would!"

"But the sprink…"

"Come on, Sher! Let's go!"

I relaxed and let my hands lose a little in this moment, excited at the thought that Stretch really wanted me to go with him, when all the sudden…

Whoosh!

Before I even knew what happened, my swim top was stripped off my body. My jaw dropped and I was so stunned that I didn't even think to put my hands up and cover myself.

"She needs some sunscreen first, fellas," stated Big Henry. I looked up at him with eyes as big as saucers, and he winked and whispered in my ear…

"Now they'll never forget who you are, kiddo!"

I couldn't decide if I wanted to faint, scream, cry or run. So I ran. I yanked my top from out of Big Henry's hands and ran inside as fast as I could yellin' out, "Go without me!"

All the boys were still standin' around, kinda stunned at what had happened, yet also not carin' one lick about it. It only mattered to me. Within seconds they were back on their bikes and headin' out for a soda and I was inside in my bedroom, huddled at the foot of my bed.

A few seconds later the door creaked opened and Stretch walked in. I wiped a fresh tear from my face and looked up.

"You… you didn't go?" I asked weakly.

"Of course not! Did you think I would go without you and leave you here to run in the sprinkler alone?"

I let out a small smile. Stretch really did have a beautiful soul.

"Of course he wouldn't! And neither would I," said Big Henry as he crept in from behind the door. "Forgive me?" he raised an eye brow as if to ask the question ten times over.

I laughed.

"If you get me a blue popsicle."

"Deal!"

And just like that I had forgotten about the whole mess. I had forgotten, and Big Henry was right. Those boys never forgot who I was.

CHAPTER 2

It was my turn to speak. Big Henry handed me the mic, sayin, "You're up, Sheryl. You know she's listenin."

I tried to turn it down, there was no way I could talk into that thing with Aunt Dee smilin' at me like that, but it was the tears in Big Henry's smile that made me go on. He looked at me in a way that my soul could feel his warmth—and those tears—they glistened as if they were smilin' too. They gave me courage. I grabbed the mic, twisted the cord around my hand, and stared into the eyes of hundreds of people waitin' for me to share my best memory, favorite recipe, or long-lost photograph I found of Aunt Dee teachin' me to play the piano. Well, to their surprise, and mine, somethin' much different came out of my mouth.

"I was sixteen when Aunt Dee gave me the worst advice anyone had ever given me."

As the words left my mouth, Big Henry choked on his own spit and let out a loud cough. I startled and dropped the mic. It crashed against the cold, wooden floor me and Big Henry was standin' on and sounded so loud you'd of thought it was a bowlin' ball. Before the crash ended, I looked Big Henry in eye, afraid I said somethin' wrong, or that I shouldn't go on. I turned my back on the eyes and ran for the stairs. Before I could get far, I ran right into a brick wall. A brick wall of muscular arms, the smell of dusty raindrops, and a warm flannel shirt. Right away, I knew.

"St…Stretch. You're…here?" I could hardly get the words out.

"I wouldn't miss my own mama's funeral, Sher. I'd regret that forever. Kinda like you'll regret droppin' that mic and walkin' out if I let you."

His grip loosened and Aunt Dee's only son looked me straight in the eye. Instead of feeling his warmth though, like I could with Big Henry, Stretch brought out my warmth. I nodded. He was right. I bent over and picked up the mic. My hands automatically went to wrappin' the cord back around my sweaty fingers, and I held it up so close to my mouth I could taste the metal. I took a deep breath and exhaled, forgettin' I had the mic stuffed in my mouth. Another loud noise rang across the speakers, and I quickly pulled back. It didn't faze a single person. They all kept starin' at me. Anxious for my words.

"I…I was sixteen years old when Aunt Dee gave me the worst advice she had ever given me…"

CHAPTER 3

I remember the exact color of blue the sky was the day I ran down Aunt Dee's mile long driveway to show her my prize possession. My driver's license. I had just turned sixteen and passed my driver's test on the first try, makin' my daddy a bit of a nervous wreck.

"Aunt Dee! Aunt Dee!" I hollered as I came crashin' in through the screen door.

"My goodness, child, slow down. Ain't you ever heard that the fastest way to get something done is by doin' it slower?"

"Aunt Dee, I passed my driver's test! I can drive! Want to go for some ice cream? Or to Freeman's for a candy bar?"

"Did you just hear one word I said, child?"

I plopped down in a chair and let the sweat pour down my face. It was the middle of July in the middle of nowhere, Mississippi, and not a day went by where every single soul didn't lose five pounds just from sweatin'.

"Yeah, yeah, I heard you, Aunt Dee. Slower is faster, I know. I know! Now can I take you for ice cream?"

She laughed her deep, rumblin' laugh while she wiped gooey bread dough from her hands.

"Yes, child, I would love to let you take me for some ice cream."

"Yes! Come on, let's go. Let's go, Aunt Dee!" I was smilin' so big I swear my cheeks were screamin' at me. I hadn't got to drive anyone anywhere yet, but I knew I wanted my first trip to be with Aunt Dee since it couldn't be with my mama. Seven years ago, when I was only nine years old—the day after Big Henry stripped me to my drawers in front of those teenage boys—was the day I have lived my life trying to forget.

It was a Sunday, my favorite day of the week. Mama always made us breakfast on Sundays. She said it was just to keep our tummies from growlin' in church, but I think it was just cause' she loved to cook pancakes for my daddy. There were few things in life my daddy loved more than pancakes and a cold glass of fresh squeezed orange juice. So every Sunday I would sit at the kitchen table and squeeze oranges til' I thought my hands would be stained forever while my mama sang hymns and cooked perfectly round pancakes. Then after breakfast, Mama and I would walk to church holding our Bibles in one hand and each other's hand in the other. We would walk to church and Daddy would go help Uncle

Jim with whatever odd chore needed done for the day. Lookin' back, I sure wish Daddy would have come to church with us a few times. At least on the days where Pastor Randy talked about forgiveness.

That particular Sunday morning I had just sliced my first orange in half when my mama let out a frustrate sign at the fridge' door

"Oh goodness… how did I let this happen?"

She slammed the fridge door shut and it was clear somethin' was wrong.

"What is it, Mama?"

"Oh nothin', just that your silly mama let us run outta milk again. A woman can't make pancakes without milk, Sher! Don't ever forget that."

I raised an eyebrow and giggled a little.

"Why does it matter if I ever forget that or not?"

Mama laughed.

"Because you'll be a mama too someday my darlin', and I hope you'll make your family pancakes on Sundays before you walk your little munchink's off to church too!"

The very thought of me ever being a mama made part of me laugh and the other part of me nearly cry. If I were a mama, would I still be my mama's little girl? I didn't want to ever think about not sittin' at the kitchen table with my own mama, and stayin' up late together watchin' *I Love Lucy* reruns. If I was a mama, what would happen to my mama? The thought put so much pressure on my chest that I ended up blurtin' it out.

"But, Mama! If I'm raisin' my own kids what is gonna happen to you?"

The sincerity of the concern in my voice startled even myself, so I can't imagine what my mama was thinkin' when I asked this question.

She tilted her head, gave a small grin, and wrapped her arms around me tight.

"Oh honey, I will still be your mama! I will just be enjoyin' the days on the porch with your daddy until we're old and gray haired when you're a mama. And I'll be playin' with my grandkids, of course!"

Her reassuring words made me feel a little better, but only for a minute. Soon enough Mama was letting me go and rememberin' that she didn't have milk.

"Well, Sher, it looks like we might have to skip the pancakes this mornin'."

The very thought of not havin' pancakes on our Sunday morning together made my eyes swell, my chest beat fast, and though I didn't mean for it to—my voice loud.

"What! No, Mama, we *have* to have pancakes!" I yelled out.

Just as I yelled my daddy walked in to the kitchen, which was quickly fallin' apart.

"What in the world is goin' on in here, girl? What's wrong?"

His tone of voice told me he was somewhat concerned, but also somewhat mad that I had raised my voice at Mama, so I decided to take the whiney approach instead.

"Daddy, we have to have pancakes, we just have to. It won't be the same if we don't!" I said in the saddest voice I could muster up.

My daddy was slightly confused, and I could tell the thought of us not havin' pancakes alarmed him a little too.

"Cait, what is she talkin' about?" he asked.

"Oh hun, I'm so sorry. I didn't get enough milk at the store this week and we're out. I don't have any milk to make pancakes.

"See, Daddy! It's a disaster!" I yelled once more. My daddy shot me a look and I quickly ducked down in my chair and shut my mouth. He did still have a concerned look on his face though, and that was my only hope.

"Now, Sheryl, just calm down. It ain't the end of the world. Either I can run into town and get a carton of milk at the gas station, or we can just live without them today. Alright?"

"But, Daddy—"

"No buts about it young lady, one day without pancakes won't kill you."

I sank deeper into my chair and tried to hold in the tears. He was right, it wasn't the end of the world. But for whatever reason it sure felt like it.

"Oh this is all my fault!" my mom yelled out.

"Cait, this is not your fault. It's fine. It's only pancakes! I can go into town…"

"No, no, no. You already have Jim waitin' on you. I'll run into town, grab a carton of milk and we will just have a late breakfast today and skip church. You make sure you let Jim know he's comin' for pancakes…"

Before Daddy could say anything Mama was already grabbin' her keys and headin' out the door.

My chest started beatin' again, but this time with excitement. We were still gonna have pancakes! My daddy tried to stop my mama one final time as she headed out the door, but before he could get one foot on the gravel she was already pullin' away. I ran outside and waved goodbye to her—the world's biggest smile on my face. My daddy looked down at me and shook his head in a playful way.

"You always get what you want, don't you, little lady?"

He ruffled my hair and walked off to his pick-up. That was the last time my daddy ruffled my hair.

"She left for milk, and never made it back home, Sheryl…" That's all he would ever tell me. I know it was a car crash, but I don't know how it happened. My daddy would never tell me, but I also never bothered to ask him, or anyone else for that matter. My mama was gone; that was all that mattered. That, and the fact that it was my fault she was gone. My daddy never forgave me for wantin' pancakes so bad, and I slowly started believin' it was my fault too. Aunt Dee was the only one who helped me let go of that thought once in a while. Sometimes late at night when I couldn't sleep cause' the pain was so bad, I would sneak outta the house and run as fast as I could to Aunt Dee's. She never locked the door at night, so I would come runnin' in through the front door, a sweaty mess with tears streamin' down my face, and she would just hold me. She would hold me tight on their livin' room couch and tell me over and over again, *"Ain't no one's job but God's to take a life…"*

I have a hard time remembering what her voice, my mama's that is, sounds like sometimes, but I will never forget how beautiful she was. I keep a picture of her tucked away in my underwear drawer and I look at it every night before I got to bed. I may not remember what Mama's voice sounded like—but I will never, ever forget her lovely smile. My daddy wouldn't give me the picture at first, so it took it from his wallet one night when he was sleepin'. I know he knows I took it, but I also know he let me keep it. He's too mad at me to even ask for the picture back. He's still too angry to admit she's gone; to forgive me.

Because my daddy had such a hard time with my mama dyin', Aunt Dee stepped in to help raise me in the years when I needed a mama most. Every mornin' Stretch would come to my door with two biscuits, an apple, and a container a' butter from Aunt Dee. We'd sit together, Stretch and I, and eat our feast, then set off back to his house where Aunt Dee would watch us on the long summer days when the sun didn't set until the men on the river decided it was time to quit fishin'. Nice woman, mother nature, lettin' those men fish for so long.

Stretch and I loved watchin' em'. We'd lay out in the sand on the river bank and dig our toes into the soil until we finally hit a patch wet enough to cool our feet. It amazed me, still does, how the sun doesn't disappear until the last man wades his way outta the water, stringer in one hand, pole in the other. Then when the last man left and the sun went to bed, Stretch and I would walk hand in hand back to Aunt Dees where she'd cook us popcorn on the stove and tell us stories til' we couldn't keep our eyes open no more. Some nights I'd get so tired, Aunt Dee and Daddy would let me stay over. I'd fall asleep next to Stretch, snugglin' up to his flannel shirt he'd let me hold and soakin' in his scent—saw dust and rain. Those nights were my favorite. Those nights are what made Aunt Dee more my mama than anyone ever had been. I know my daddy loved me, and he tried real hard, but there were times when only Aunt Dee could fix the pain.

CHAPTER 4

"Aunt Dee, come on! You're takin' forever!" I ran out to the car, jumped in, and reached over to unlock the passenger door. I honked the horn twice, and Aunt Dee finally appeared at the doorway.

"Girl, if you honk that horn one more time I'm gonna turn around and go knit me a different hat to wear right this minute!"

I lowered my head and pressed it against the steering wheel, tryin' to hide my laughter from Aunt Dee. One thing's for sure, she lived—and died—by the motto, "Slower is faster." She loved to stop and pick flowers on any walk we ever took, and always made it especially painful when we was tryin' to get to the river to fish. "Sheryl and Stretch, you two listen," she'd say, "if you don't stop and smell the flowers on the path of life, you ain't gonna experience any life at all. And if you ain't okay with dyin', you won't either. Life's about livin' eternally, not materially…"

About that time her voice would drift off and Stretch and I would start runnin' toward the river again. Neither of us was too sure what that meant at the time anyway, but we'd just smile and agree, lettin' Aunt Dee pick all the flowers she wanted. Worst part was, they always died by the time we got home anyway. What was the point of pickin' all those flowers?

Right then Aunt Dee finally made it to the car, I had finally stopped laughin'.

"Can we go now?" I asked, anxiety climbing high in my voice.

"Yes," Aunt Dee breathed out, "we can go."

I cranked the key, fired up the ignition, and slammed my foot down on the gas. We were off to get ice cream, me and Aunt Dee...

CHAPTER 5

The next thing I remember, there were sirens piercing my ears, everything around me was black, and when I moved my fingers I could feel dead brush beneath my hands. "Am I dreamin'? what's happenin'?" I had no idea where I was or what was goin' on, all I knew was that if I kept my eyes closed, it had to be a dream. It had to be a dream, and I would wake up. I would wake up and Aunt Dee would be sittin' in the seat next to me, singing Amazing Grace and talkin' about which ice cream flavors we were gonna get. So I kept my eyes closed. Hard.

"Excuse me, ma'am? Are you awake?"

Don't move, Sheryl. It's a dream. He isn't real.

"If you can hear me, can you respond? We need to know if you're conscious, ma'am."

Suddenly such a sharp pain tore through my back I knew there was no way I could be dreamin'. I let out a scream and opened my eyes. I wasn't prepared to take in everythin' around me. There was broken glass, blood, clothes, my wallet, my mama… it was everywhere.

"What happened?" I yelled, wrestling to stand up.

"Ma'am, we need you to…"

"Where's Aunt Dee? Aunt Dee!"

"Ma'am!" One of the men in a fire suit yelled, grabbed my arm and pulled me up and close to his body. "I need you to calm down, and let me take you to an ambulance. We need to get you on a stretcher."

I let him continue to hold me close, but the confusion didn't go away.

"Where's Aunt Dee! Tell me!"

All I could remember was changing the radio, talkin' about ice cream, and comin' up on… the… the four way stop. That was it. That was all I could remember.

"Ma'am listen to me, I'm gonna need to get your information so we can get ahold of your parents while we get you onto a stretcher. Can you tell me your name?"

"Let me see her."

"Ma'am…"

"Let. Me. See. Her." I talked more slowly this time, making my demand very clear.

He wrapped his arms back around me and led me around the corner to the second ambulance. That's when I knew. I saw Aunt Dee, strapped to the bed, covered in blankets, oxygen mask tied down to her fast, chest not beatin'.

"Aunt Dee?"

Silence.

"I think she may be conscience for another few minutes, but then we'll probably lose her. You can go talk to her if you'd like.. but please, I'd rather you come with me…"

I pushed him aside and walked toward the stretcher. "Aunt Dee?"

"Sheryl? Is that you? My darlin' little girl?"

There was blood smeared across her face. Her right eye had swollen shut, and her left eye brow looked as though it had been cut from her face. I stopped breathin'.

"Oh, look at you! You look so much like your mama."

I exhaled one slow, deep breath.

"Aunt Dee…I'm, I'm so sorry…"

I had no idea what to say.

"Oh hush, child. I'm fine…" she exhaled slowly and made a horrible wheezing sound. "I get to see Jesus soon, and you know what?"

The mention of Jesus sent chills through my blood and caused me to burst into tears. Fire went through me.

"No! No, Aunt Dee, you can't die!"

"You know what, child?"

I fell to my knees and buried my head in my hands, tears streamin' down my face. The weak look on Aunt Dee's face was already burning itself into my mind. I was fallin' apart, but she kept goin'…

"You're gonna forget all about this night, you are. You're gonna grow up to be as beautiful as your mama, and you're gonna keep eatin' ice cream. You know why?"

The tears came harder now. She was still here. Still talking. She wouldn't die, right? People don't talk like this when they are about to die—it's just not possible.

"Why is no one helping her!" I cried. I stood up and stepped closer. "Aunt Dee, you're gonna be all right. They're gonna get you help. It'll be ok. Someone, help!"

It was then that I saw it. The branch that was pierced through her body, holding her together.

"Do you know why you gonna keep on eatin' ice cream, child?"

I backed away. I couldn't breathe again.

"Cause you ain't just like your mama, you're also just like me. You stop to smell the flowers. You slow down when you goin' places, and you know you gotta be ok with death to be able to live, because death doesn't win—Jesus does. So be okay with death, okay child? You gotta be ... okay ... with ..."

Her eyes drifted shut. The fireman pulled me back into his arms and there was nothing but cold surrounding my body. No thoughts. No words. Just cold.

"I really need to get you to an ambulance now."

I couldn't move. If he wanted to take me anywhere, he was gonna have to carry me. I was done.

Chapter 6

"Three days later, I'm standin' here at Aunt Dee's funeral tellin' you what she told me. That I have to be okay with death. That was her advice. Her last words."

The eyes still stared, fixed on my face, entranced in my words. I could tell no one was understandin' what I was tryin' to say, so I knew it was time to wrap things up. I had finally relived both my mama and Aunt Dee's death, and it somehow made me feel better. Rememberin' Aunt Dee's words… *"Jesus wins…"* I knew I could learn to forgive myself. It might take time, but I could do it. Stretch was standin' next to me now. He wrapped his fingers around mine and placed a soft hand on my shoulder. He knew he didn't need to say anything, but just simply be there. I took a deep breath and tried to finish what seemed to be an endless speech.

"It's the worst advice she ever gave me. She told me to stop and smell the flowers—and I will. She told me to go slower—and I will. But I won't be okay with death. I will only be okay with rememberin' the life she lived, and livin' every day the best I can until I see her again

in heaven. Because death doesn't win—Jesus does. Jesus forgives me, Aunt Dee forgives me, and I hope someday my daddy can forgive me. Just like how someday I will see Aunt Dee smilin', hear her laughin', and give her a scoop of vanilla ice cream."

From the back row, I heard a light cough and saw a figure stir. I looked up and saw my daddy standin' up, starin' right at me—with a small smile makin' its way across his face.